Playing Hockey

Chuck Solomon

CROWN PUBLISHERS, INC.
New York

For Jeff Gingold

Acknowledgments: Thanks very much to the North Park Hockey Association: John Stickney, President; coaches Eric Huckaby, Pete Suozzo, and Scott Bommer, and all the great players.

Published by Crown Publishers, Inc., a Random House company, 225 Park Avenue South, New York, New York 10003
CROWN is a trademark of Crown Publishers, Inc.

Manufactured in Hong Kong.

Library of Congress Cataloging-in-Publication Data
Solomon, Chuck. Playing hockey
Summary: Follows, in text and photographs, young ice hockey players as they practice and play on outdoor ponds and in city leagues.
1. Hockey—Juvenile literature. 2. [1. Hockey.] I. Title.
GV848.4.U6S65   1990   796.96′2′0974—dc20   89-1031

ISBN 0-517-57414-4
      0-517-57415-2 (lib. bdg.)

10 9 8 7 6 5 4 3 2 1
First Edition

In winter when it's cold outside, hockey players head for the pond.

The ice has to be thick enough before it's safe to skate on. Everyone helps sweep and scrape the snow off the ice.

We set up our goals—two boots, a stick length apart.

Good friends who live nearby keep extra skates handy. We can swap skates we've outgrown for skates that fit just right.

When everyone is ready, play begins. "Don't lift the puck!" one of the older players reminds us. We play without protective equipment, so the puck can only be shot along the ice.

On these cold days, everyone stays warm by skating and playing hard.

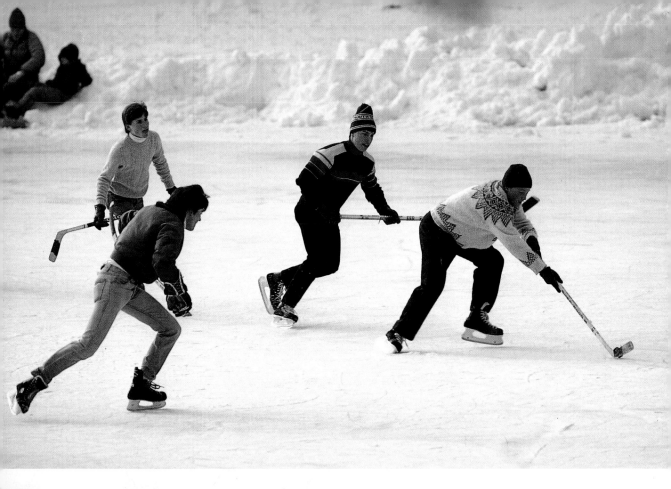

As more people come
to the pond they join in.
Everyone plays. We don't
keep score; we just love
playing hockey for the
fun of it.

We play until we can
barely see the puck as
the sun goes down in the
late afternoon.

Then it's time to put
our equipment away
and tape any broken
sticks to get ready for
the next day's skate.

Kids in the city love to play hockey too.

Our hockey rink has refrigeration pipes underneath to keep the ice frozen.

A Zamboni ice resurfacer scrapes the ice smooth and leaves a layer of water. When the water freezes, the ice is even and fast.

Our goal is made of metal pipe and netting.

We wear full protective equipment. Our padding, gloves, and headgear help protect us from falls, speeding pucks, and stray hockey sticks.

Our coaches tell us to line up in single file for drills.

"Cut it close!" Scott says as he shows
us how to skate around the pylons.

"Skate backward on your way back," Eric tells us. "Keep that puck in front of you and look straight ahead!"

Hockey players have to learn how to skate backward, especially when we're on defense.

Peter tells us to break into pairs and try passing the puck back and forth as we head toward the goal.

Then we practice our shooting. Line up those shots—first a slap shot and then a wrist shot.

Our goaltenders practice too. They're reminded that they can stop the puck with their skates, pads, stick, or glove.

Goaltenders have to react quickly to stop a speeding puck.

Soon it is time for a game. The coach divides
us into groups. The Flames play against the
Rangers. Peter explains that we are going to
play in three-minute shifts and that everyone
will get into the game.

The puck is dropped
for the face-off to
start the match.

Hockey is a fast game! The puck and skaters
travel quickly up and down the ice.

Sometimes we take a hard spill but we pick ourselves up and get right back into the game.

While the game goes full speed, other players wait their turn to get on the ice.

Each team scores a goal
and we're tied at one just
before we take a break.

Break time!
  Even on a freezing day we work up a thirst for a cool drink.

We hit the ice again.

Both goalies make fine stops. Players
from both benches shout "Great save!"

Everyone skates hard
and tries to score
in the last few minutes
of the contest.

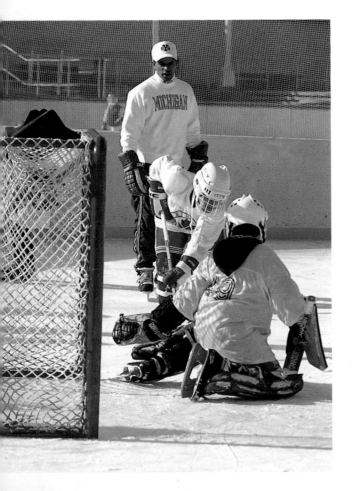

With just a minute left the Rangers score again and the game ends. The Rangers win two to one.

In the spirit of good
sportsmanship, both
teams line up to shake
hands when the game
is over.

After a day of skating and shooting the puck, we really get tired out. It's time for a good sleep and to think about playing again next Saturday.